THIS BOOK
BELONGS TO:

_____

_____

_____

For Anna
M.W.

For Sebastian,
David & Candlewick
H.O.

Published by arrangement with Walker Books Ltd, London SE11 5HJ

Dual language edition first published 2006 by Mantra Lingua
Dual language TalkingPEN edition first published 2010 by Mantra Lingua
Global House, 303 Ballards Lane, London N12 8NP, UK
http://www.mantralingua.com

Text copyright © 1991 Martin Waddell
Illustrations copyright © 1991 Helen Oxenbury
Dual language text and audio copyright © 2006 Mantra Lingua
This edition 2015

A CIP record of this book is available from the British Library

Printed in Paola, Malta MP251115PB12150399

鴨子農夫
FARMER DUCK

written by
MARTIN WADDELL

illustrated by
HELEN OXENBURY

Mantra Lingua

從前有一隻鴨子，牠很不幸地與一個懶惰的老農夫一起住。
鴨子要做所有的工作，而農夫則整天懶臥在床上。

There once was a duck who had the bad luck
to live with a lazy old farmer.
The duck did the work.
The farmer stayed
all day in bed.

鴨子從耕地把牛拉回。
「工作做得怎樣？」農夫叫道，
鴨子回答說：
「嘎！」

The duck fetched the cow from the field.
"How goes the work?"
called the farmer.
The duck answered,
"Quack!"

鴨子從山丘上把羊群帶領回來。
「工作做得怎樣？」農夫叫道，
鴨子回答說：
「嘎！」

The duck brought the sheep from the hill.
"How goes the work?" called the farmer.
The duck answered,
"Quack!"

鴨子把雞隻們趕回牠們的雞屋。
「工作做得怎樣？」農夫叫道，
鴨子回答說：
「嘎！」

The duck put the hens in their house.
"How goes the work?"
called the farmer.
The duck answered,
"Quack!"

農夫由於整天睡覺而變得肥胖，
可憐的鴨子則因爲整天工作而逐漸感到厭煩。

The farmer got fat through staying in bed
and the poor duck got fed up
with working all day.

「工作做得怎樣？」
「嘎！」

"How goes the work?"
"QUACK!"

「工作做得怎樣？」
「嘎！」

"How goes the work?"
"QUACK!"

「工作做得怎樣？」
「嘎！」

"How goes the work?"
"QUACK!"

「工作做得怎樣？」
「嘎！」

"How goes the work?"
"QUACK!"

「工作做得怎樣？」
「嘎！」

"How goes the work?"
"QUACK!"

「工作做得怎樣？」
「嘎！」

"How goes the work?"
"QUACK!"

可憐的鴨子淚汪汪的，
又疲乏，又想睡。

The poor duck was sleepy
and weepy
and tired.

雞隻們、羊群和牛都感到很不安，
牠們都喜愛鴨子，
於是牠們便在月亮下開了一個會，
為第二天的早晨作好計劃。

「哞！」牛說，
「咩！」羊群說，
「咯！」雞隻們說。
那便是牠們的計劃了。

The hens and the cow
and the sheep got very
upset.
They loved the duck.
So they held a meeting
under the moon and
they made a plan
for the morning.

"MOO!" said the cow.
"BAA!" said the sheep.
"CLUCK!" said the hens.
And THAT was the plan!

就在清晨之前，農場還很靜寂，
牛、羊群、以及雞隻們悄悄地從後門走進屋子。

It was just before dawn and the farmyard was still.
Through the back door and into the house
crept the cow and the sheep and the hens.

牠們偷偷地走過門堂，
吱吱嘎嘎地爬上樓梯。

They stole down the hall.
They creaked
up the stairs.

牠們擠到農夫的床底下扭動，
那張床開始搖擺，農夫醒過來叫道：
「工作做得怎樣？」
跟著…

They squeezed under the bed of
the farmer and wriggled about.
The bed started to rock and the
farmer woke up, and he called,
"How goes the work?"
and…

「哞！」
「咩！」
「咯！」

"MOO!"
"BAA!"
"CLUCK!"

牠們將床擡起，農夫開始大聲地叫喊，
牠們敲撞著，把農夫拋來拋去，
將他從床上拋彈下來…

They lifted his bed and he started to shout, and they banged
and they bounced the old farmer about and about and about,
right out of the bed...

農夫逃跑去了，牛、羊群、以及雞隻們跟著他，
圍著他哞呀、咩呀、咯呀地叫。

and he fled with the cow and the sheep and the hens mooing and baaing and clucking around him.

沿著小路…
「哞！」

Down the lane…
"Moo!"

穿過田間…
「咩！」

through the fields…
"Baa!"

越過山丘…
「咯！」

over the hill...
"Cluck!"

他再也不回來了。

and he never came back.

鴨子醒來後，蹣跚地走進農場，
以為會聽到「工作做得怎樣？」
但沒有人說一句話！

The duck awoke and waddled wearily into the yard expecting
to hear, "How goes the work?"
But nobody spoke!

跟著牛、羊群、以及雞隻們都回來了。
「嘎？」鴨子問道，
「哞！」牛說，
「咩！」羊群說，
「咯！」雞隻們說。
牠們將整件事告訴鴨子。

Then the cow and the sheep and the hens came back.
"Quack?" asked the duck.
"Moo!" said the cow.
"Baa!" said the sheep.
"Cluck!" said the hens.
Which told the duck
the whole story.

牠們跟著便哞呀、咩呀、
咯呀和嘎呀地到農場工作去。

Then mooing and baaing
and clucking and quacking
they all set to work
on their farm.